The Little Fox

The Little Fox

AN ALASKA ADVENTURE

Written and Illustrated by Ram Papish

SNOWY OWL BOOKS

an imprint of the University of Alaska Press

SNOWY OWL BOOKS
an imprint of the University of Alaska Press

University of Alaska Press
P.O. Box 756240
Fairbanks, AK 99775-6240

Library of Congress Cataloging-in-Publication Data

Papish, Ramiel.
   The little fox : an Alaska adventure / by Ram Papish.
      p. cm.
Summary: Little Fox is carried by a piece of the melting ice pack to a
rocky island in Alaska's Bering Sea, where he spends a year observing
various plants, birds, and animals while searching for food and traces
of other arctic foxes.
   ISBN-13: 978-1-889963-87-7 (board book : alk. paper)
   ISBN-10: 1-889963-87-9 (board book : alk. paper)
1. Arctic fox—Juvenile fiction. [1. Arctic fox—Fiction. 2. Foxes—Fiction.
3. Animals—Alaska—Fiction. 4. Islands—Fiction. 5. Alaska—Fiction.] I. Title.
   PZ10.3.P22245Lit 2007
   [Fic]—dc22
                              2006006837

This publication was printed on acid-free paper that meets the minimum
requirements for ANSI/NISO Z39.48–1992 (R2002) (Permanence of Paper
for Printed Library Materials).

Printed in China

About the Author and Illustrator

*Ram (pronounced "Rom") Papish
graduated from the University of Oregon
in 1995 with degrees in art and biology
and has worked as a field biologist all
over the Western Hemisphere.
He has studied nesting seabirds on
several remote islands in Alaska and
draws upon his experiences as a
biologist and birder to produce beautiful
and accurate wildlife paintings.*

Each spring the great northern pack ice
breaks apart, sending its frozen pieces southward.

This year, an arctic fox falls asleep on the edge of the
ice. He had been following a polar bear, scavenging
on the scraps of seal meat she left behind.

Little Fox awakens to find himself floating on a great
chunk of ice in the dark green waters of Alaska's mighty
Bering Sea. And the ice is melting beneath him.

The ice melts away to nearly nothing. Little
Fox sees the small dark shape of an island
in the distance.

Should he jump into the icy waters and swim?
The tiny iceberg bobs and bobs.

His toes are getting wet.

Little Fox plunges in! Swimming, swimming he reaches the barren, rocky shore of the island. He hauls himself up. He shakes off the cold. Pshh, shahh…. The only sound is the gentle slapping of waves lapping against the shore. He sees no sign of life.

Starving, Little Fox sniffs between the slippery rocks. He finds bits to eat. The leg of a crab. The tail of a fish.

What is this? Out of the frozen ground grows a single flowering stalk. It is a Chukchi primrose sending out a soft circle of violet petals. Little Fox goes to sleep beside it. He is very alone in this cold world of sea and stone.

Little Fox awakes to a gray dawn. He sees a northern
fur seal lying asleep beside him!

The great, grizzled seal swam north from the distant
Gulf of Alaska to claim his spot on the rocky shore.

One tired eye opens, just a crack, and Little
Fox runs away. Will he find another fox in this
land of cold, wet rocks?

As he scurries down the shoreline, Little Fox hears the chittering, chattering sound of ten thousand tiny birds. Chubby least auklets buzz around his head like oversized bumble bees. He has never seen so many birds!

They land on the rocks. He pounces after one— but it slips into the dark crack between two boulders. These birds know how to disappear! Has a fox hunted here before?

Little Fox hears the sound of chattering voices from deep beneath the immovable stone. Now loud, now soft, the raspy calls of the colony rise and fall in unison: chur chur chur ER ER ER chur chur chur.

Little Fox nimbly climbs the cliffs, smelling a salty mix of fish and guano from the white-washed stone.

He hears barking, then the strange sound of a honking horn: onk Onk ONK HONK! He turns to see the bent-back head and fan-shaped crest of a bugling auklet. Another crested auklet throws back his head and honks.

Females look on, trying to decide who will be the best mate. Which one has the biggest crest? From the bugling birds comes the unfamiliar scent of some far-off land. These auklets smell like fruit!

Little Fox hears a rhythmic sound:
tu tu tu EH EH EH tu tu tu.
Slow, fast, slow.

The parakeet auklet's oddly hooked
beak is just right for catching
jellyfish and floating shrimp.

One bird crawls into a crack
where it lays a single
white egg.

The sun sinks below the horizon for only a few hours. WHAK WHAK Kitti Whak!

Little Fox awakens to the loud cries of two black-legged kittiwakes flying in on great white wings tipped with black.

One has a mouthful of dry yellow grass, and the other calls its name: KIT ti WAKE! KIT ti WAKE!

Another pair of kittiwakes cries back from their nest: Kit It WAK AK AK. The harsh sound pierces the moist, salty air.

13

Little Fox hears sounds from below: hard, loud sounds of roaring and soft, gentle sounds of ba-ba-bahing. A strong smell like sun-baked seaweed and old crab claws draws the fox forward.

The rocky shore is covered with the twisting forms of a thousand fur seals! He sees a great, grizzled male towering silently above the many barking females and baying pups.

The great eye of the beachmaster rolls from side to side, alert for any sign of other males approaching. Only the beachmaster and no other seal will mate with the females around him.

Then Little Fox smells death. Some pups don't get enough milk. Some males die from fighting. Little Fox will have no trouble scavenging for food on the rocky shores of his island.

Days of plenty pass. Little Fox climbs the cliffs. The ground of cold gray dirt is covered now with greens and golds, purples and pastels, lupine and lousewort, weasel-snout and sea-pink. The gentle breeze brings the sweet smell of bluebells and the tinkling sound of longspur song.

Bright-billed birds, the clown-faced puffins land high on the cliffs and search for cavities in which to nest.

The tufted puffin has tufts of creamy yellow.
The horned puffin has horns of darkest black.

One puffin nests early...
one puffin nests late.

One brings a beak full of
flowers to line its nest. One
brings a beak full of fish to
feed its hungry chick.

Down underground is the
sound of deep purring.
Errrrr... er er er er....

Murrrrr ... urr urr. From the narrow cliffs below comes the moaning, groaning, grumbling sound of the common murre.

Gur gur arrrrr, answers the white-whiskered thick-billed murre.

Pear-shaped eggs lie on shelves of stone with no nest to hold them. Why don't they roll off? When bumped the great green egg rolls in a circle.

Little Fox will not get an easy meal here.

From every nook and cranny, from every crack, crevice, corner and shelf come the chirps, honks, gurgles, squeaks, barks, and roars of the island's inhabitants.

23

As the days shorten so do the crests, tufts, whiskers, and wispy white plumes of the seabirds. Little Fox sees them changing into winter plumage.

The full-grown chicks test their wings.

The seals swim off to distant seas.

Will they ever return?

The nights grow long. The air grows cold. The wind whistles day after dark day. Little Fox is alone.

His fur grows long and thick. Snow blankets the island. He has trouble finding food. Neither the leg of a crab nor the tail of a fish is left for him to gnaw on. Little Fox finds a skull that could have been his own.

The great northern pack ice creeps closer every day. He finds a fish head washed in on the waves. He catches a worm wiggling in a tidepool.

He survives the darkest days of winter.

27

Day after day passes. The sun stays longer now. The ice begins to break up…. And what is this?

Little Fox sees something swimming, swimming toward him from the shattering sheet of ice. A pale shape hauls itself onto the barren island of rock. It shakes off the cold. Sniffing the gentle breeze, he finds the familiar smell of a female fox.

He walks on tippy toes toward her with his tail raised straight up, trying to look big. She crouches on the ground and lays back her ears, trying to look small. He nips at her nose and backs away. She follows. Little Fox is no longer alone!

As the snow melts, a Chukchi primrose sends up its circle of purple petals. Spring has come again! The hungry foxes will soon find plenty of food on their distant island of rock.

As the island grows green and spring turns to summer, a first litter of foxes opens its eyes to a bright new world.

Proceeds from the sale of this book will support the Pribilof Islands Stewardship Program. This summer camp program is administered by the St. George Traditional Council, P.O. Box 940, St. George Island, AK 99591.

The philosophy of the program is that the Pribilof Islands are our home; so is the world. We are interconnected, thus everything we do produces effects that we must acknowledge and be aware of now.

The vision of the program is to encourage protectorship, awareness, and responsibility for our home islands and the Bering Sea, which includes sharing these responsibilities with others.

The Pribilof fox (*Alopex lagopus pribilofensis*) is a unique subspecies of arctic fox that differs in its form, behavior, and genetics from arctic foxes anywhere else in the world. It is not known exactly when foxes colonized the Pribilof Islands, but they were abundant when the Russians arrived in 1786. Three-thousand-year-old fox bones have been found on St. George Island.

Arctic foxes occur in two distinct colors known as "blue" and "white." "Blue" foxes are uniformly dark year-round, but change from a dull brown in summer to a darker slaty blue-brown in winter. "White" foxes are pure white during the snowy winter months, with a two-toned brown and creamy white coat in the summer. Most of the foxes on the Pribilof Islands represent the "blue" phase.

The arctic fox has evolved to live in the most frigid extremes on the planet. Among its adaptations for surviving the cold are a short muzzle and small, rounded ears to reduce heat loss. Their bodies are covered with thick, dense fur coats—the densest of any land mammal. In winter, fur grows over the pads of the foxes' feet. Coupled with a specialized circulatory system in their paws, this fur helps protect them from the ice and snow. To further insulate them from the cold and help them survive the long winters when food is scarce, arctic foxes store enough fat each fall to nearly double their body weight.

Arctic foxes mate from early March to early April. The gestation period is fifty-two days. Litters of island foxes tend to be smaller (average five pups) than on the mainland (up to fifteen pups). Both the mother and the father help to raise the young. In the fall, young of both sexes disperse on the mainland. However, on the Pribilof Islands, foxes often form larger family groups, with yearlings staying on to help their parents raise next year's young.

Foxes travel far from land out onto the ice in search of food and listen for movements of prey beneath the snow. Although their appetites are notably diverse, Pribilof foxes eat mostly seabirds and their eggs as well as dead seals, lemmings, shellfish, and fish. Pribilof foxes measure 85 to 105 cm total length (about three feet from nose to the tip of the tail) with a summer weight between 3 and 5 kg (about 11 pounds).

Dr. Paula A. White
University of California, Berkeley